Moving on Sand and Snow

Written by Jo Windsor

Rigby

The camel is in the desert.
Look at its feet.
Its feet will not go down
into the sand.

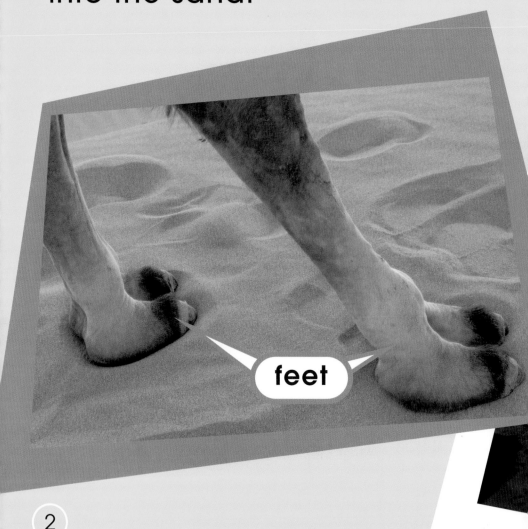

feet

This car is in the desert, too. Its wheels will not go down into the sand.

wheels

4

This lizard is in the desert.
Look at its feet.
It has webbed feet.
Its feet will not go down
into the sand.

feet

This rabbit is in the snow.
It has fur on its feet.
Its feet will not go down
into the snow.

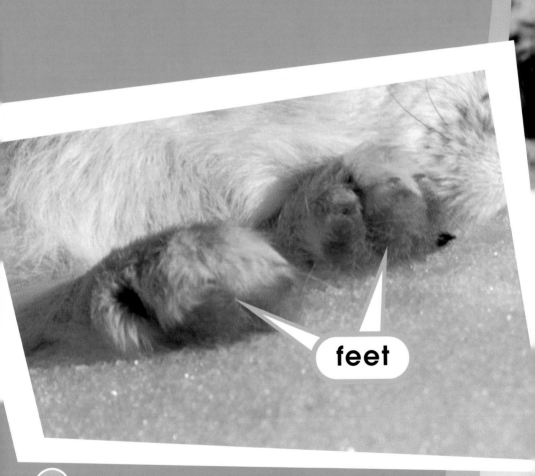

feet

This bird is in the snow, too.
This bird has feathers
on its feet.
Its feet will not go down
into the snow.

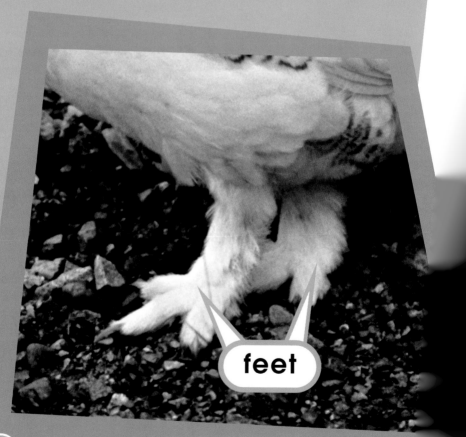

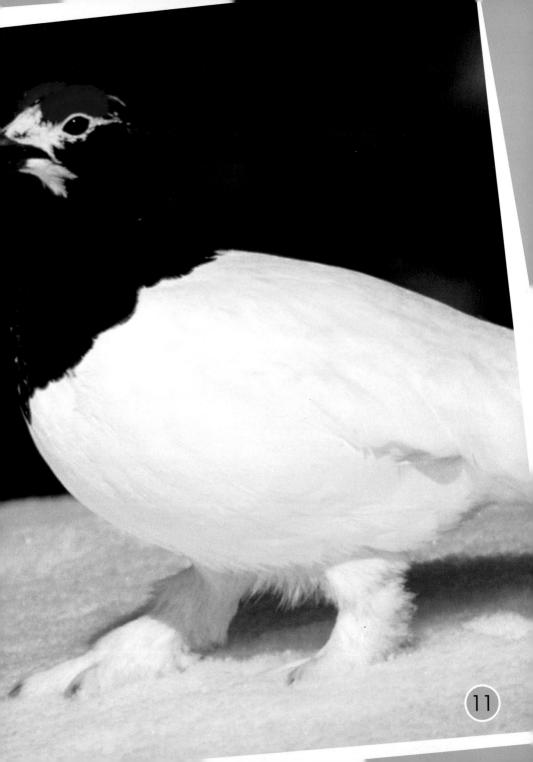

This man is in the snow.
Look at his feet.
His feet will not go down
into the snow.

feet

13

Index

Guide Notes

Title: Moving on Sand and Snow
Stage: Early (2) – Yellow

Genre: Nonfiction
Approach: Guided Reading
Processes: Thinking Critically, Exploring Language, Processing Information
Written and Visual Focus: Photographs (static images), Labels, Index
Word Count: 121

THINKING CRITICALLY
(sample questions)
- Tell the children this book is about different ways animals and people can move on sand and snow.
- Look at the title and read it to the children.
- Ask the children what they know about how we can move across sand and snow.
- Focus the children's attention on the index. Ask: "What are you going to find out about in this book?"
- If you want to find out about a lizard, on which page would you look?
- If you want to find out about a bird, on which page would you look?
- What is different about the feet on pages 7 and 8?
- What else do you think a rabbit might use its feet for?
- Why do you think the wheels on the car will not go down into the sand?

EXPLORING LANGUAGE

Terminology
Title, cover, photographs, author, photographers

Vocabulary
Interest words: camel, desert, sand, wheels, webbed, snow, fur, feathers
High-frequency word: its
Positional words: into, down, in, on

Print Conventions
Capital letter for sentence beginnings, periods, commas